ESCAPE FROM PLANET ALCATRAZ

THE CRUSHING CRYSTALS

BY MICHAEL DAHL

ILLUSTRATED BY SHEN FEI

STONE ARCH BOOKS

a capstone imprint

Escape from Planet Alcatraz is published by
Stone Arch Books
A Capstone Imprint
1710 Roe Crest Drive
North Mankato, Minnesota 56003
www.capstonepub.com

Library of Congress Cataloging-in-Publication Data
Names: Dahl, Michael, author. | Fei, Shen (Illustrator), illustrator.
Title: The crushing crystals / by Michael Dahl ; illustrated by Shen Fei.
Description: North Mankato, MN : Stone Arch Books, a Capstone
  imprint, [2020] | Series: Escape from planet Alcatraz
Identifiers: LCCN 2019005617 (print) | LCCN 2019009645 (ebook) |
  ISBN 9781496583239 (eBook PDF) | ISBN 9781496583161
  (library binding)
Subjects: LCSH: Science fiction. | Prisons—Juvenile fiction. | Escapes—
  Juvenile fiction. | Extraterrestrial beings—Juvenile fiction. | Extrasolar
  planets—Juvenile fiction. | Adventure stories. | CYAC: Science
  fiction. | Prisons—Fiction. | Escapes—Fiction. | Extraterrestrial
  beings—Fiction. | Adventure and adventurers—Fiction. | LCGFT:
  Science fiction. | Action and adventure fiction.
Classification: LCC PZ7.D15134 (ebook) | LCC PZ7.D15134 Ct 2020
  (print) | DDC 813.54 [Fic]—dc23
LC record available at https://lccn.loc.gov/2019005617

Summary: Zak Nine and his alien friend, Erro, are trying to make it
across the Plateau of Leng before the robot guards of planet Alcatraz can
find them. But as the sun rises, mountain-sized crystals suddenly start
rising around them through the desert sands, threatening to trap them
with a giant, deadly scorpion. Will the boys figure out how to escape
this series of dangerous threats?

Editor: Aaron J. Sautter
Designer: Kay Fraser
Production Specialist: Katy LaVigne

Design elements: Shutterstock: Agustina Camilion, A-Star, Dima Zel,
Draw_Wing_Zen, Hybrid_Graphics, Metallic Citizen

TABLE OF CONTENTS

ERRO

PLATEAU of LENG

PHANTOM FOREST

POISON SEA

VULCAN MOUNTAINS

LAKE of GOLD

METAL MOON

DIAMOND MINES

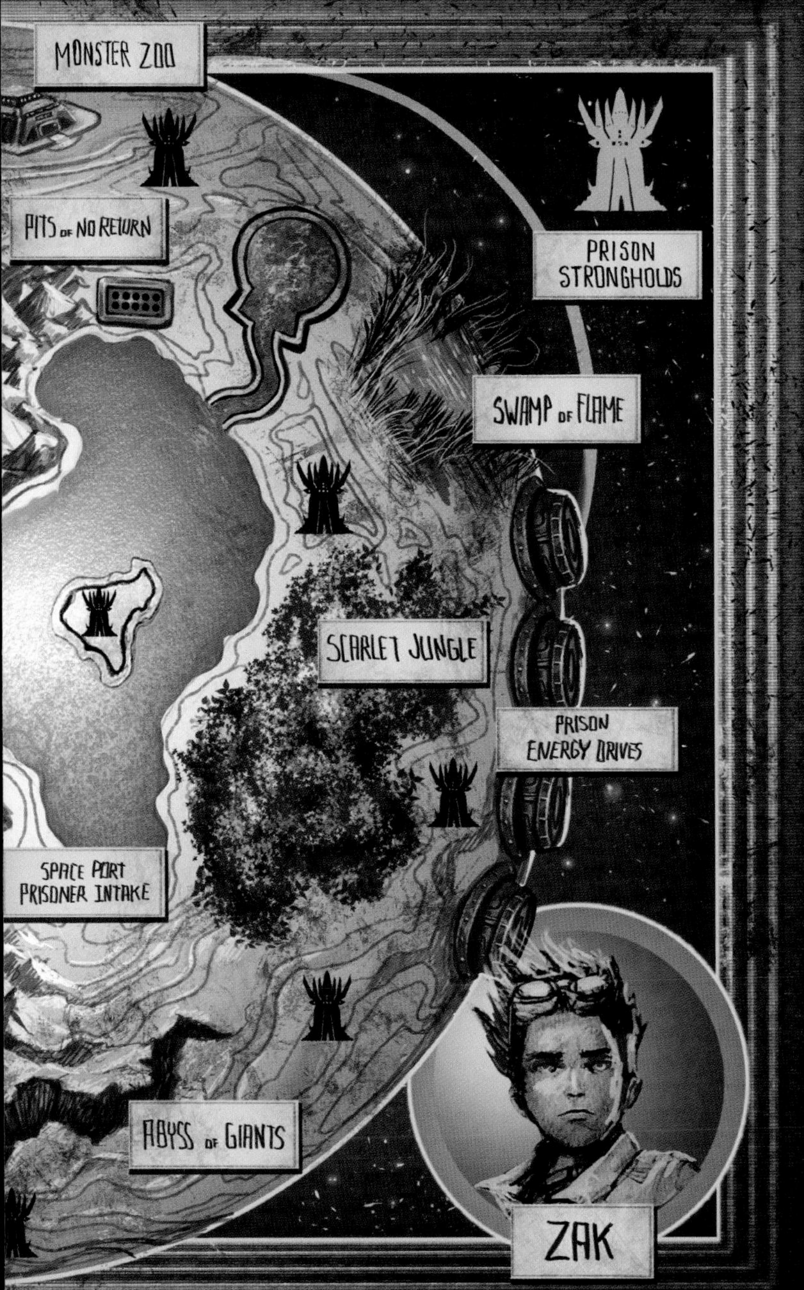
MONSTER ZOO
PITS OF NO RETURN
PRISON STRONGHOLDS
SWAMP OF FLAME
SCARLET JUNGLE
PRISON ENERGY DRIVES
SPACE PORT PRISONER INTAKE
ABYSS OF GIANTS
ZAK

THE PRISONERS

ZAK NINE

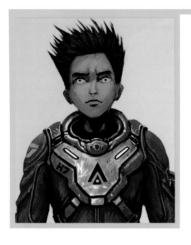

Zak is a teenage boy from Earth Base Zeta. He dreams of piloting a star fighter one day. Zak is very brave and is a quick thinker. But his enthusiasm often leads him into trouble.

ERRO

Erro is a teenage furling from the planet Quom. He has the fur, long tail, sharp eyes, and claws of his species. Erro is often impatient with Zak's reckless ways. But he shares his friend's love of adventure.

THE PRISON PLANET

Alcatraz... there is no escape from this terrifying prison planet. It's filled with dungeons, traps, endless deserts, and other dangers. Zak Nine and his alien friend, Erro, are trapped here. They had sneaked onto a ship hoping to see an awesome space battle. But the ship landed on Alcatraz instead. Now they have to work together if they ever hope to escape!

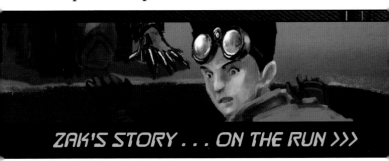

ZAK'S STORY... ON THE RUN >>>

We've been running for days through this giant desert. A few nights ago Erro and I found an electronic map device in an empty old spaceship. Erro thinks it will lead us to a safe hiding place. But I just hope we can avoid getting caught by Alcatraz's robot guards....

>>>>>

CHAPTER ONE:
THE FREEZING DARK

Alcatraz's robot guards have been trailing us for days.

The desert sky is as dark as a whomp bat. The wind bites through my thin clothes. The blowing sand feels like ice.

Erro is lucky. He's got fur. He can stay warm here on the windy plain.

But I'm freezing! All the walking
we've done hasn't warmed me up at all.

At least the map device in my hand is warm. We found it in a crashed prison ship two days ago.

"Is the device still working?" Erro asks.

"It's still glowing green," I say. I think that has to be a good sign.

Maybe the map can show us how to get across this strange, flat land.

The map calls this area the Plateau of Leng. Maybe we can cross it before the robots find us. They're only a mile away.

I don't want to see their wicked metal claws again.

A pale light is growing in the distance. The sun will be up soon. Then the guards will easily see us in this empty place.

"We need to hurry," I tell Erro.

Erro leaps across the sandy land. He can easily jump ten feet at a time. The guy acts like it's nothing.

I'm rushing to catch up. But it's not easy to read the map and run at the same time.

CHAPTER TWO:
THE PLATEAU OF LENG

Suddenly I see something on the map about the local animal life.

"Wait, Erro!" I yell out. "The map says there are scorpion rats!"

Erro stops and looks back at me. He looks scared. "Did you say . . . rats?" he asks.

At that moment, a ray of sunlight pierces the sky. We hear a loud rumble. The ground begins shaking beneath our feet.

Suddenly we hear a crash. Erro and I spin around to look behind us.

We stare in awe as a gleaming mountain shoots up from the ground. It looks like it's made of ice or glass. The jagged shapes are a rainbow of color.

"Crystal," says Erro. "A mountain of crystal!"

KRRRRRAAAAAACCKK!

Another mountain of crystal rises up next to the first one. Sand from the desert spills down its sides.

The gleaming shapes form a huge wall between us and the robot guards.

"Yes!" I shout. "Those robots won't get through that crystal wall."

The rising crystal walls grind and crush against each other. Bright chunks break off and fall to the ground.

"Look out!" cries Erro.

"What—?" I start to say. But then he shoves me to the side.

THUD!

A huge chunk of sparkling crystal lands right in front of me.

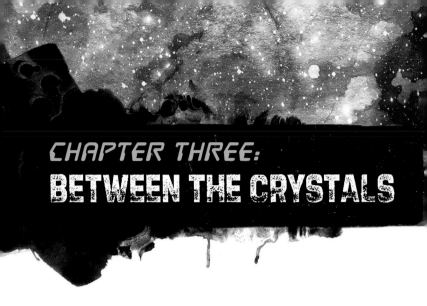

CHAPTER THREE:
BETWEEN THE CRYSTALS

The morning sun is now higher in the sky. New cliffs of crystal continue rising up around us.

"Oh no! We're being surrounded!" I shout.

"Look," Erro says, pointing. "I think it is the sun. The sunlight is making the crystals grow."

He's right. The crystals keep growing wherever rays of sunshine touch them. It looks like bubbling glass.

Then I see a narrow gap between two mountains ahead of us.

The gap between the mountains is in shadow. It should stay open if the sunlight doesn't reach it—I hope.

Erro and I run as fast as we can.

"The gap is getting smaller!"
Erro shouts. "We will not make it!"

"Oh, yes we will, fur boy!" I shout
back. "Keep running!"

Sunlight reflects off the crystal walls behind us. As the walls grow higher, the light races across the sand beside us.

Everywhere the sun touches, smaller crystals begin to bubble up.

Erro looks at me with his wide yellow eyes. We both know what will happen if the beams of sunlight reach the gap.

We race faster and faster.

CHAPTER FOUR:
A TIGHT SQUEEZE

Erro and I reach the gap and squeeze through the opening.

The walls on either side press inward on us. The sharp, glassy walls rip my clothes as we move forward.

Just as we reach the end of the passage, bright-red sunlight sparkles behind us!

KRAACKKKKKKK!

New slabs of sharp red crystal smash against each other. They fill up the gap, and the passage is gone!

"See? We made it," I say to Erro, breathing heavily.

But my alien friend's tail is twitching again. Something is wrong.

I follow his eyes and see something golden. It's rising up out of a hole in the sand.

Is that another crystal wall? I think.

No—it's a big yellow scorpion with the face of a rat!

CHAPTER FIVE:
CRACK!

We stand there, staring at the scorpion.

The wicked creature stares back, clicking its huge claws. Its deadly tail slowly rises over its body.

The sun is higher in the sky now. More crystal cliffs are rising all around us. Chunks of broken crystal fall to the ground like meteors.

CRRUUNNCH!

KRASSSSSSSHHH!

In a moment, we'll be trapped inside with the monster.

Erro suddenly looks up and then back at the scorpion. Then he starts waving his arms at the creature.

"Over here!" he shouts.

"Are you crazy?" I yell.

The scorpion skitters toward us on its clicking legs. Its ratlike mouth opens, and we see rows of sharp yellow teeth.

Erro and I back up against the crystal wall. With the gap closed, there is no escape.

When the scorpion moves closer,
Erro cups his hands around his mouth.
He tilts his head back and cries out.

SQQQQQUUUEEEEEEEEEE!

It is not a human sound.

Something rumbles high above. A large slab of crystal breaks off above our heads.

THOOOOM!!!

The broken slab of crystal falls and crushes the scorpion. Its deadly tail wiggles, and then it stops.

"Whoa! You broke that crystal with your voice," I say to Erro.

"It is a hunter's call from Quom," he says, smiling. "Sadly, it is not strong enough to open a passage through the crystal."

I step around the dead scorpion and stare down into the hole.

"That creepy-crawler came from this hole," I say. "Maybe it can lead us out."

We crawl into the dark tunnel that travels deep under the ground.

"I hope there are no more scorpions," Erro says.

"Me too," I reply. Hopefully the tunnel will lead us somewhere safe. . . .

GLOSSARY

crystal (KRISS-tuhl)—a mineral or rock with a regular pattern of many flat surfaces

device (di-VISSE)—a tool that does a particular job

dungeon (DUHN-juhn)—a prison, usually underground

meteor (MEE-tee-ur)—a piece of rock that falls from space

passage (PASS-ij)—a corridor or tunnel

plateau (pla-TOH)—an area of high, flat land

reflect (ri-FLEKT)—to return light from the surface of an object

scorpion (SKOR-pee-uhn)—an animal related to a spider with pincers and jointed tail tipped with a poisonous stinger

skitter (SKIT-ur)—to move in a quick or jerky way

species (SPEE-sheez)—a group of living things that share similar features

trail (TRAYL)—to follow the tracks or signs left behind by animals, people, or moving objects

TALK ABOUT IT

1. Zak and Erro start the story lost in a freezing sandstorm. Can you think of any ways the boys could have better protected themselves in the harsh conditions?

2. Erro noticed that sunlight caused the huge crystals to grow out of the sand. Do any crystals form that quickly on Earth? Do some research and share what you find with your friends.

3. Zak and Erro work well together to escape their situation. But what would happen if they split up? Describe what you think each boy would need to do to survive in the desert on his own.

WRITE ABOUT IT

1. This story takes place on the Plateau of Leng. How do you think this area earned its name? Write a short story that explains how the Plateau of Leng got its name.

2. Erro is frightened of scorpion rats at first. But he later finds his courage and defeats one. Write about a time when you acted bravely in spite of being scared of something.

ABOUT THE AUTHOR

Michael Dahl is the author of more than 300 books for young readers, including the bestselling Library of Doom series. He is a huge fan of Star Trek, Star Wars, and Doctor Who. He has a fear of closed-in spaces, but has visited several prisons, dungeons, and strongholds, both ancient and modern. He made a daring escape from each one. Luckily, the guards still haven't found him.

ABOUT THE ILLUSTRATOR

Shen Fei loved comic books as a child. By the age of five he began making his own comic books and drew scenes from his favorite movies. After graduating from art school he worked in the entertainment industry, creating art for film, games, and books. Shen currently lives in Malaysia and works as a freelance illustrator for publishers all over the world. He also teaches at a local art school as a guest lecturer.